I0818765

DEATH BETWEEN THE STARS

Start Publishing PD LLC

Manufactured in the United States of America

Cover art: Shutterstock/Taisiya Kozorez

Cover design: Jennifer Do

10 9 8 7 6 5 4 3 2 1

ISBN 979-8-8809-0366-5

DEATH BETWEEN THE STARS

by Marion Zimmer Bradley

They asked me about it, of course, before I boarded the starship. All through the Western sector of the Galaxy, few rules are stricter than the one dividing human from nonhuman, and the little Captain of the Vesta—he was Terran, too, and proud in the black leather of the Empire's merchant—man forces—hemmed and hawed about it, as much as was consistent with a spaceman's dignity.

"You see, Miss Vargas," he explained, not once but as often as I would listen to him, "this is not, strictly speaking, a passenger ship at all. Our charter is only to carry cargo. But, under the terms of our franchise, we are required to transport an occasional passenger, from the more isolated planets where there is no regular passenger service. Our rules simply don't permit us to discriminate, and the Theradin reserved a place on this ship for our last voyage."

He paused, and re—emphasized, "We have only the one passenger cabin, you see. We're a cargo ship and we are not allowed to make any discrimination between our passengers." He looked angry about it. Unfortunately, I'd run up against that attitude before. Some Terrans won't travel on the same ship with nonhumans even when they're isolated in separate ends of the ship.

I understood his predicament, better than he thought. The Theradin seldom travel in space. No one could have foreseen that Haalvordhen, the Theradin from Samarra, who had lived on the forsaken planet of Deneb for eighteen of its cycles, would have chosen this particular flight to go back to its own world.

At the same time, I had no choice. I had to get back to an Empire planet—any planet—where I could take a starship for Terra. With war about to explode in the Procyon sector, I had to get home before communications were knocked out altogether. Otherwise—well, a Galactic war can last up to eight hundred years. By the time regular transport service was reestablished, I wouldn't be worrying about getting home.

The Vesta could take me well out of the dangerous sector, and all the way to Samarra—Sirius Seven—which was, figuratively speaking, just across the street from the Solar System and Terra. Still, it was a questionable solution. The rules about segregation are strict, the anti—discriminatory laws are stricter, and the Theradin had made a prior reservation. The captain of the Vesta couldn't have refused him transportation, even if fifty human, Terran women had been left stranded on Deneb IV. And sharing a cabin with the Theradin was ethically, morally and socially out of the question. Haalvordhen was a non—human telepath; and no human in his right senses will get any closer than necessary even to a human telepath. As for a nonhuman one -

And yet, what other way was there?

The captain said tentatively, "We might be able to squeeze you into the crewmen's quarters—" he paused uneasily, and glanced up at me.

I bit my lip, frowning. That was worse yet. "I understand,"

I said slowly, "that this

Theradin—Haalvordhen—has offered to allow me to share its quarters."

"That's right. But, Miss Vargas—"

I made up my mind in a rush. "I'll do it," I said. "It's the best way, all around."

At the sight of his scandalized face, I almost regretted my decision. It was going to cause an interplanetary scandal, I thought wryly. A human woman—and a Terran citizen—spending forty days in space and sharing a cabin with a nonhuman!

The Theradin, although male in form, had no single attribute which one could remotely refer to as sex. But of course that wasn't the problem. The nonhuman were specifically prohibited from mingling with the human races. Terran custom and taboo were binding, and I faced, resolutely, the knowledge that by the time I got to Terra, the planet might be made too hot to hold me.

Still, I told myself defiantly, it was a big Galaxy. And conditions weren't normal just now and that made a big difference. I signed a substantial check for my transportation, and made arrangements for the shipping and stowing of what few possessions I could safely transship across space.

But I still felt uneasy when I went aboard the next day—so uneasy that I tried to bolster up my flagging spirits with all sorts of minor comforts. Fortunately the Theradin were oxygen—breathers, so I knew there would be no trouble about atmosphere—mixtures, or the air pressure to be maintained in the cabin. And the Theradin were Type Two nonhumans, which meant that the acceleration of a hyperspeed ship would knock my shipmate into complete prostration without special drugs. In fact, he would probably stay drugged in his skyhook during most of the trip.

The single cabin was far up toward the nose of the starship. It was a queer little spherical cubbyhole, a nest. The walls were foam—padded all around the sphere, for passengers never develop a spaceman's skill at maneuvering then: bodies in free—fall, and cabins had to be designed so that an occupant, moving unguardedly, would not dash out his or her brains against an unpadded surface. Spaced at random on the inside of the sphere were three skyhooks—nested cradles on swinging pivots—into which the passenger was snugged during blastoff hi shock—absorbing foam and a complicated Garensen pressure—apparatus and was thus enabled to sleep secure without floating away.

A few screw—down doors were marked LUGGAGE. I immediately unscrewed one door and stowed my personal belongings in the bin. Then I screwed the top down securely and carefully fastened the padding over it. Finally, I climbed around the small cubbyhole, seeking to familiarize myself with it before my unusual roommate arrived.

It was about fourteen feet in diameter. A sphincter lock opened from the narrow corridor to cargo bays and crewmen's quarters, while a second led into the cabin's functional equivalent of a bathroom. Planet—bound men and women are always surprised and a little shocked when they see the sanitary arrangements on a spaceship. But once they've tried to perform normal bodily functions in free—fall, they understand the peculiar equipment very well.

I've made six trips across the Galaxy in as many cycles. I'm practically an old hand, and can even wash my face in freefall without drowning. The trick is to use a sponge and suction. But, by and large, I understand perfectly why spacemen, between planets, usually look a bit unkempt.

I stretched out on the padding of the main cabin, and waited with growing uneasiness for the nonhuman to show. Fortunately, it wasn't long before the diaphragm on the outer sphincter lock expanded, and a curious, peaked face peered through.

"Vargas Miss Helten?" said the Theradin in a sibilant whisper.

"That's my name," I replied instantly. I pulled upward, and added, quite unnecessarily, "You are Haalvordhen, of course."

"Such is my identification," confirmed the alien, and the long, lean, oddly—muscled body squirmed through after the peaked head. "It is kind, Vargas Miss, to share accommodation under this necessity."

"It's kind of you," I said vigorously. "We've all got to get home before this war breaks out!"

"That war may be prevented, I have all hope," the nonhuman said. He spoke comprehensibly in Galactic Standard, but expressionlessly, for the vocal chords of the Theradins are located in an auxiliary pair of inner lips, and their voices seem reedy and lacking in resonance to human ears.

"Yet know you, Vargas Miss, they would have hurled me from this ship to make room for an Empire citizen, had you not been heart—kind to share."

"Good heavens!" I exclaimed, shocked, "I didn't know that!" I stared at him, disbelieving. The captain couldn't have legally done such a thing—or even seriously have entertained the thought. Had he been trying to intimidate the Theradin into giving up his reserved place?

"I—I was meaning to thank you," I said, to cover my confusion.

"Let us thank we—other, then, and be in accord," the reedy voice mouthed. I looked the nonhuman over, unable to hide completely my curiosity. In form the Theradin was vaguely humanoid—but only vaguely—for, the squat arms terminated in mittened "hands" and the long sharp face was elfin, and perpetually grimacing.

The Theradin have no facial muscles to speak of, and no change of expression or of vocal inflection is possible to them. Of course, being telepathic, such subtleties of visible or auditory expression would be superfluous on the face of it.

I felt—as yet—none of the revulsion which the mere presence of the Theradin was supposed to inspire. It was not much different from being in the presence of a large humanoid animal. There was nothing inherently fearful about the alien. Yet he was a telepath—and of a nonhuman breed my species had feared for a thousand years. Could he read my mind?

"Yes," said the Theradin from across the cabin. "You must forgive me. I try to put up barrier, but it is hard. You broadcast your thought so strong it is impossible to shut it out." The alien paused. "Try not to be embarrass. It bother me too."

Before I could think of anything to say to that a crew member in black leather thrust his head, unannounced, through the sphincter, and said with an air of authority, "In skyhooks, please." He moved confidently into the cabin. "Miss Vargas, can I help you strap down?" he asked.

"Thanks, but I can manage," I told him.

Hastily I clambered into the skyhook, buckling the inner straps, and fastening the suction tubes of the complicated Garensen apparatus across my chest and stomach. The nonhuman was awkwardly drawing his hands from their protective mittens and struggling with the Garensens.

Unhappily the Theradin have a double thumb, and handling the small—size Terran equipment is an almost impossibly delicate task. It is made more difficult by the fact that the flesh of their "hands" is mostly thin mucous membrane which tears easily on contact with leather and raw metal.

"Give Haalvordhen a hand," I urged the crewman. "I've done—this dozens of times!" I might as well have saved my breath. The crewman came and assured himself that my straps and tubes and cushions were meticulously tightened. He took what seemed to me a long time, and used his hands somewhat excessively, I lay under the heavy Garensen equipment, too inwardly furious to even give him the satisfaction of protest.

It was far too long before he finally straightened and moved toward Haalvordhen's skyhook. He gave the alien's outer straps only a perfunctory tug or two, and then turned his head to grin at me with a totally uncalled—for—familiarity.

"Blastoff in ninety seconds," he said, and wriggled himself rapidly out through the hook. Haalvordhen exploded in a flood of Samarran which I could not follow. The vehemence of his voice, however, was better than a dictionary. For some strange reason I found myself sharing his fury. The unfairness of the whole procedure was shameful. The Theradin had paid passage money, and deserved in any case the prescribed minimum of decent attention.

I said forthrightly, "Never mind the fool, Haalvordhen. Are you strapped down all right?"

"I don't know," he replied despairingly. "The equipment is unfamiliar—"

"Look—" I hesitated, but in common decency I had to make the gesture. "If I examine carefully my own Garensens, can you read my mind and see how they should be adjusted?"

He mouthed, "I'll try," and immediately I fixed my gaze steadily on the apparatus. After a moment, I felt a curious sensation. It was something like the faint, sickening feeling of being touched and pushed about, against my will, by a distasteful stranger. I tried to control the surge of almost physical revulsion. No wonder that humans kept as far as possible from the telepathic races. . .

And then I saw—did I see, I wondered, or was it a direct telepathic interference with my perceptions?—a second image superimpose itself on the Garensens into which I was strapped. And the realization was so disturbing that I forgot the discomfort of the mental rapport completely.

"You aren't nearly fastened in," I warned. "You haven't begun to fasten the suction tubes—oh, damn the man. He must have seen in common humanity—" I broke off abruptly, and fumbled in grim desperation with my own straps. "I think there's just time—"

But there wasn't. With appalling suddenness a violent clamor—the final warning—hit my ears. I clenched my teeth and urged frantically: "Hang on! Here we go!"

And then the blast hit us! Under the sudden sickening pressure I felt my lungs collapse, and struggled to remain upright, choking for breath. I heard a queer, gagging grunt from the alien, and it was far more disturbing than a human scream would have been.

Then the second Shockwave struck with such violence that I screamed aloud in completely human terror. Screamed—and blacked out.

I wasn't unconscious very long. I'd never collapsed during takeoff before, and my first fuzzy emotion when I felt the touch of familiar things around me again was one of embarrassment. What had happened? Then, almost simultaneously, I became reassuringly aware that we were in free fall and that the crewman who had warned us to alert ourselves was stretched out on the empty air near my skyhook. He looked worried.

"Are you all right, Miss Vargas?" he asked, solicitously. "The blastoff wasn't any rougher than usual—"

"I'm all right," I assured him woozily. My shoulders jerked and the Garensens shrieked as I pressed upward, undoing the apparatus with tremulous fingers. "What about the Theradin?" I asked urgently. "His Garensens weren't fastened. You barely glanced at them."

The crewman spoke slowly and steadily, with a deliberation I could not mistake. "Just a minute, Miss Vargas," he said. "Have you forgotten? I spent every moment of the time I was in here fastening the Theradin's belts and pressure equipment." He gave me a hand to assist me up, but I shook it off so fiercely that I flung myself against the padding on the opposite side of the cabin. I caught apprehensively at a handhold, and looked down at the Theradin.

Haalvordhen lay flattened beneath the complex apparatus. His peaked pixie face was shrunken and ghastly, and his mouth looked badly bruised. I bent closer, then jerked upright with a violence that sent me cascading back across the cabin, almost into the arms of the crewman.

"You must have fixed those belts just now," I said accusingly. "They were not fastened before blastoff! It's malicious criminal negligence, and if Haalvordhen dies—" The crewman gave me a slow, contemptuous smile. "It's my word against yours, sister," he reminded me.

"In common decency, in common humanity—" I found that my voice was hoarse and shaking, and could not go on. The crewman said humorlessly, "I should think you'd be glad if the geek died in blastoff. You're awfully concerned about the geek—and you know how that sounds?"

I caught the frame of the skyhook and anchored myself against it. I was almost too faint to speak. "What were you trying to do?" I brought out at last. "Murder the Theradin?"

The crewman's baleful gaze did not shift from my face. "Suppose you close your mouth," he said, without malice, but with an even inflection that was far more frightening. "If you don't, we may have to close it for you. I don't think much of humans who fraternize with geeks."

I opened and shut my mouth several times before I could force myself to reply. All I finally said was, "You know, of course, that I intend to speak to the captain?"

"Suit yourself." He turned and strode contemptuously toward the door. "We'd have been doing you a favor if the geek had died in blastoff. But, as I say, suit yourself. I think your geek's alive, anyhow. They're hard to kill."

I clutched the skyhook, unable to move, while he dragged his body through the sphincter lock and it contracted behind him.

Well, I thought bleakly, I had known what I would be letting myself in for when I'd made the arrangement. And since I was already committed, I might as well see if Haalvordhen were alive or dead. Resolutely I bent over his skyhook, angling sharply to brace myself in free—fall.

He wasn't dead. While I looked I saw the bruised and bleeding "hands" flutter spasmodically. Then, abruptly, the alien made a queer, rasping noise. I felt helpless and for some reason I was stirred to compassion.

I bent and laid a hesitant hand on the Garensen apparatus which was now neatly and expertly fastened. I was bitter about the fact that for the first time hi my life I had lost consciousness! Had I not done so the crewman could not have so adroitly covered his negligence. But it was important to remember that the circumstance would not have helped Haalvordhen much either.

"Your feelings do you nothing but credit!" The reedy flat voice was almost a whisper. "If I may trespass once more on your kindness—can you unfasten these instruments again?"

I bent to comply, asking helplessly as I did so, "Are you sure you're all right?"

"Very far from all right," the alien mouthed, slowly and without expression.

I had the feeling that he resented being compelled to speak aloud, but I didn't think I could stand that telepath touch again. The alien's flat, slitted eyes watched me while I carefully unfastened the suction tubes and cushioning devices.

At this distance I could see that the eyes had lost their color, and that the raw "hands" were flaccid and limp. There were also heavily discolored patches about the alien's throat and head. He pronounced, with a terribly thick effort: "I should have—been drugged. Now it's too late. Argha mad—" the words trailed off into blurred Samarran, but the discolored patch in his neck still throbbed sharply, and the hands twitched in an agony which, being dumb, seemed the more fearful.

I clung to the skyhook, dismayed at the intensity of my own emotion. I thought that Haalvordhen had spoken again when the sharp jolt of command sounded, clear and imperative, in my brain.

"Procalamine!" For an instant the shock was all I could feel—the shock, and the overwhelming revulsion at the telepathic touch. There was no hesitation or apology in it now, for the Theradin was fighting for his life. Again the sharp, furious command came: "Give me procalamine!"

And with a start of dismay I realized that most nonhumans needed the drug, which was kept on all spaceships to enable them to live in free—fall.

Few nonhuman races have the stubbornly persistent heart of the Terrans, which beats by muscular contraction alone. The circulation of the Theradin, and similar races, is dependent on gravity to keep the vital fluid pulsing. Procalamine gives their main blood organ just enough artificial muscular spasm to keep the blood moving and working.

Hastily I propelled myself into the "bathroom"—wiggled hastily through the diaphragm, and unscrewed the top of the bin marked FIRST AID. Neatly pigeonholed beneath transparent plastic were sterile bandages, antiseptics clearly marked HUMAN and—separately, for the three main types of nonhuman races, in one deep bin—the small plastic globules of vital stimulants.

I sorted out two purple fluorescent ones—little globes marked procalamine— and looked at the warning, in raised characters on the globule. It read: FOR ADMINISTRATION BY QUALIFIED SPACE PERSONNEL ONLY. A touch of panic made my diaphragm catch. Should I call the Vesta's captain, or one of the crew?

Then a cold certainty grew in me. If I did, Haalvordhen wouldn't get the stimulant he needed. I sorted out a fluorescent needle for nonhuman integument, pricked the globule and sucked the dose into the needle. Then, with its tip still enclosed in the plastic globe, I wriggled myself back to where the alien still lay loosely confined by one of the inner straps.

Panic touched me again, with the almost humorous knowledge that I didn't know where to inject the stimulant, and that a hypodermic injection in space presents problems which only space—trained men are able to cope with. But I reached out notwithstanding and gingerly picked up one of the unmittened "hands." I didn't stop to think how I knew that this was the proper site for the injection. I was too overcome with strong physical loathing.

Instinct from man's remote past on Earth told me to drop the nonhuman flesh and cower, gibbering and howling as my simian antecedents would have done. The raw membrane was feverishly hot and unpleasantly slimy to touch. I fought rising queasiness as I tried to think how to steady him for the injection.

In free—fall there is no steadiness, no direction. The hypodermic needle, of course, worked by suction, but piercing the skin would be the big problem. Also, I was myself succumbing to the dizziness of no—gravity flight, and realized coldly that if I couldn't make the injection in the next few minutes I wouldn't be able to accomplish it at all. For a minute I didn't care, a primitive part of myself reminding me that if the alien died I'd be rid of a detestable cabin mate, and have a decent trip between planets.

Then, stubbornly, I threw off the temptation. I steadied the needle in my hand, trying to conquer the disorientation which convinced me that I was looking both up and down at the Theradin.

My own center of gravity seemed to be located in the pit of my stomach, and I fought the familiar space voyaging instinct to curl up in the foetal position and float. I moved slightly closer to the Theradin. I knew that if I could get close enough, our two masses would establish a common center of gravity, and I would have at least a temporary orientation while I made the injection.

The maneuver was unpleasant, for the alien seemed unconscious, flaccid and still, and mere physical closeness to the creature was repellent. The feel of the thick wettish "hand" pulsing feebly in my own was almost sickeningly ultimate. But at last I managed to maneuver myself dose enough to establish a common center of gravity between us—an axis on which I seemed to hover briefly suspended.

I pulled Haalvordhen's "hand" into this weight—center in the bare inches of space between us, braced the needle, and resolutely stabbed with it.

The movement disturbed the brief artificial gravity, and Haalvordhen floated and bounced a little weightlessly in his skyhook. The "hand" went sailing back, the needle recoiling harmlessly. I swore out loud, now quite foolishly angry, and my own jerky movement of annoyance flung me partially across the cabin.

Inching slowly back, I tried to grit my teeth, but only succeeded with a snap that jarred my skull. In tense anger, I seized Haalvordhen's "hand," which had almost stopped its feverish pulsing, and with a painfully slow effort—any quick or sudden movement would have thrown me, in recoil, across the cabin again—I wedged Haalvordhen's "hand" under the strap and anchored it there.

It twitched faintly—the Theradin was apparently still sensible to pain—and my stomach rose at that sick pulsing. But I hooked my feet under the skyhook's frame, and flung my free arm down and across the alien, holding tight to the straps that confined him. Still holding him thus wedged down securely, I jabbed again with the needle. It touched, pricked—and then, in despair, I realized it could not penetrate the Theradin integument without weight and pressure behind it.

I was too absorbed now in what had to be done to care just how I did it. So I wrenched forward with a convulsive movement that threw me, full—length, across the alien's body. Although I still had no weight, the momentum of the movement drove the hypodermic needle deeply into the flesh of the "hand."

I pressed the catch, then picked myself up slowly, and looked around to see the crewman who had jeered at me with his head thrust through the lock again, regarding me with the distaste he had displayed toward the Theradin, from the first. To him I was lower than the Theradin, having degraded myself by close contact with a nonhuman.

Under that frigid, contemptuous stare, I was unable to speak. I could only silently withdraw the needle and hold it up. The rigid look of condemnation altered just a little, but not much. He remained silent, looking at me with something halfway between horror and accusation.

It seemed years, centuries, eternities that he clung there, just looking at me, his face an elongated ellipse above the tight collar of his black leathers. Then, without even speaking, he slowly withdrew his head and the lock contracted behind him, leaving me alone with my sickening feeling of contamination and an almost hysterical guilt. I hung the needle up on the air, curled myself into a ball, and, entirely unstrung, started sobbing like a fool.

It must have been a long time before I managed to pull myself together, because before I even looked to see whether Haalvordhen was still alive, I heard the slight buzzing noise which meant it was a meal—period and that food had been sent through the chute to our cabin. I pushed the padding listlessly aside, and withdrew the heat—sealed containers—one set colorless, the other set nonhuman fluorescent.

Tardily conscious of what a fool I'd been making of myself, I hauled my rations over to the skyhook, and tucked them into a special slot, so that they wouldn't float away. Then, with a glance at the figure stretched out motionless beneath the safety—strap of the other skyhook, I shrugged, pushed myself across the cabin again, and brought the fluorescent containers to Haalvordhen.

He made a weary, courteous noise which I took for acknowledgment. By now heartily sick of the whole business, I set them before him with a bare minimum of politeness and withdrew to my own skyhook, occupying myself with the always—ticklish problem of eating m free—fell.

At last I drew myself up to return the containers to the chute, knowing we wouldn't leave the cabin during the entire trip. Space, on a starship, is held to a rigid minimum. There is simply no room for untrained outsiders moving around in the cramped ship, perhaps getting dangerously close to critically delicate equipment, and the crew is far too busy to stop and keep an eye on rubbernecking tourists.

In an emergency, passengers can summon a crewman by pressing a call—button. Otherwise, as far as the crew was concerned, we were in another world.

I paused in midair to Haalvordhen's skyhook. His containers were untouched and I felt moved to say, "Shouldn't you try to eat something?"

The flat voice had become even weaker and more rasping now, and the nonhuman's careful enunciation was slurred. Words of his native Samarran intermingled with queer turns of phrase which I expected were literally rendered from mental concepts.

"Heart—kind of you, thakkava Varga Miss, but late. Haalvordhen—I deep in grateful wishing—" A long spate of Samarran, thickly blurred followed, then as if to himself, "Theradin—we, die nowhere only on Samarra, and only a little tune ago Haalvordhen—I knowing must die, and must returning to home planet. Saata. Knowing to return and die there where Theradin—we around dying—" The jumble of words blurred again, and the limp "hands" clutched spasmodically, in and out.

Then, in a queer, careful tone, the nonhuman said, "But I am not living to return where I can stop—die. Not so long Haalvordhen—I be lasting, although Vargas—you Miss be helping most like real instead of alien. Sorry your people be most you unhelping—" he stopped again, and with a queer little grunting noise, continued, "Now Haalvordhen—I be giving Vargas—you stop—gift of heritage, be needful it is."

The flaccid form of the nonhuman suddenly stiffened, went rigid. The drooping lids over the Theradin's eyes seemed to unhood themselves, and in a spasm of fright I tried to fling myself backward. But I did not succeed. I remained motionless, held in a dumb fascination.

I felt a sudden, icy cold, and the sharp physical nausea crawled over me again at the harsh and sickening touch of the alien on my mind, not in words this time, but in a rapport even closer—a hateful touch so intimate that I felt my body go limp in helpless fits and spasms of convulsive shuddering under the deep, hypnotic contact.

Then a wave of darkness almost palpable surged up in my brain. I tried to scream, "Stop it, stop it!" And a panicky terror flitted in my last conscious thought through my head. This is why, this is the reason humans and telepathy don't mix -

And then a great dark door opened under my senses and I plunged again into unconsciousness.

It was not more than a few seconds, I suppose, before the blackness swayed and lifted and I found myself floating, curled helplessly in mid—air, and seeing, with a curious detachment, the Theradin's skyhook below me. Something in the horrid limpness of that form stirred me wide awake.

With a tight band constricting my breathing, I arrowed downward. I had never seen a dead Theradin before, but I needed no one to tell me that I saw one now. The constricting band still squeezed my throat in dry gasps, and in a frenzy of hysteria I threw myself wildly across the cabin, beating and battering on the emergency button, shrieking and sobbing and screaming. . .

They kept me drugged all the rest of the trip. Twice I remember waking and shrieking out things I did not understand myself, before the stab of needles in my arm sent me down into comforting dreams again. Near the end of the flight, while my brain was still fuzzy, they made me sign a paper, something to do with witnessing that the crew held no responsibility for the Theradin's death.

It didn't matter. There was something clear and cold and shrewd in my mind, behind the surface fuzziness, which told me I must do exactly what they wanted, or I would find myself in serious trouble with the Terran authorities. At the time I didn't even care about that, and supposed it was the drugs. Now, of course, I know the truth.

When the ship made planetfall at Samarra, I had to leave the Vesta and transship for Terra. The Vesta's little captain shook me by the hand and carefully avoided my eyes, without mentioning the dead Theradin. I had the feeling—strange, how clear it was to my perceptions—that he regarded me in the same way he would regard a loaded time bomb that might explode at any moment.

I knew he was anxious to hurry me aboard a ship for Terra. He offered me special reservations on a lino-cruiser at a nominal price, with the obvious lie that he owned a part interest in at. Detachedly I listened to his floundering lies, ignored the hand he offered again, and told a lie or two of my own. He was angry. I knew he didn't want me to linger on Samarra.

Even so, he was glad to be rid of me.

Descending at last from the eternal formalities of the Terran landing zone, I struck out quickly across the port city and hailed a Theradin ground—car. The Theradin driving it looked at me curiously, and in a buzzing voice informed me that I could find a human conveyance at the opposite corner. Surprised at myself, I stopped to wonder what I was doing. And then -

And then I identified myself in a way the Theradin could not mistake. He was nearly as surprised as I was. I clambered into the car, and he drove me to the queer, block—shaped building which my eyes had never seen before, but which I now knew as intimately as the blue sky of Terra.

Twice, as I crossed the twisting ramp, I was challenged. Twice, with the same shock of internal surprise, I answered the challenge correctly.

At last I came before a Theradin whose challenge crossed mine like a sure, sharp lance, and the result was startling. The Theradin Haalvamphrenan leaned backward twice in acknowledgment, and said—not in words—"Haalvordhen!"

I answered in the same fashion. "Yes. Due to certain blunders, I could not return to our home planet, and was forced to use the body of this alien. Having made the transfer unwillingly, under necessity, I now see certain advantages. Once within this body, it does not seem at all repulsive, and the host is highly intelligent and sympathetic.

"I regret the feeling that I am distasteful to you, dear friend. But, consider. I can now contribute my services as messenger and courier, without discrimination by these mind—blind Terrans. The law which prevents Theradin from dying on any other planet should now be changed."

"Yes, yes," the other acquiesced, quickly grasping my meaning. "But now to personal matters, my dear Haalvordhen. Of course your possessions are held intact for you."

I became aware that I possessed five fine residences upon the planet, a private lake, a grove of Theirry-trees, and four chattel boats. Inheritance among the Theradin, of course, is dependent upon continuity of the mental personality, regardless of the source of the young. When any Theradin died, transferring his mind into a new and younger host, the new host at once possessed all of those things which had belonged to the former personality. Two Theradin, unsatisfied with their individual wealth, sometimes pooled their personalities into a single host—body, thus accumulating modest fortunes.

Continuity of memory, of course, was perfect. As Helen Vargas, I had certain rights and privileges as a Terran citizen, certain possessions, certain family rights, certain Empire privileges. And as Haalvordhen, I was made free of Samarra as well.

In a sense of strict justice, I "told" Haalvamphrenan how the original host had died. I gave him the captain's name. I didn't envy him, when the Vesta docked again at Samarra.

"On second thought," Haalvamphrenan said reflectively, "I shall merely commit suicide in his presence."

Evidently Helen—Haalvordhen—I had a very long and interesting life ahead of me.

So did all the other Theradin.

www.ingramcontent.com/pod-product-compliance
Lightning Source LLC
Chambersburg PA
CBHW030416310726
48979CB00002B/442

* 9 7 9 8 8 8 0 9 0 3 6 6 5 *